P9-CCX-779

two lions

Text copyright © 2010, Dallas Clayton
All rights reserved.
Printed in China

Published by Two Lions, New York
www.apub.com
Amazon, the Amazon Logo, and Two Lions are trademarks
of Amazon.com, Inc., or its affiliates.

The characters and events portrayed in this book are fictitious. Any
similarity to real persons, living or dead, is coincidental and not
intended by the author.

No part of this book may be reproduced, or stored in a retrieval
system, or transmitted in any form or by any means, electronic,
mechanical, photocopying, recording, or otherwise, without express
written permission of the publisher.

ISBN-13: 978-1-935597-37-7
ISBN-10: 1-935597-37-X

Produced by Awesome World, LLC
550 North Larchmont Boulevard
Suite 201
Los Angeles, California 90004

Cover and interior design and illustration by Dallas Clayton

two lions

Text copyright © 2010, Dallas Clayton
All rights reserved.
Printed in China

Published by Two Lions, New York
www.apub.com
Amazon, the Amazon Logo, and Two Lions are trademarks
of Amazon.com, Inc., or its affiliates.

The characters and events portrayed in this book are fictitious. Any
similarity to real persons, living or dead, is coincidental and not
intended by the author.

No part of this book may be reproduced, or stored in a retrieval
system, or transmitted in any form or by any means, electronic,
mechanical, photocopying, recording, or otherwise, without express
written permission of the publisher.

ISBN-13: 978-1-935597-37-7
ISBN-10: 1-935597-37-X

Produced by Awesome World, LLC
550 North Larchmont Boulevard
Suite 201
Los Angeles, California 90004

Cover and interior design and illustration by Dallas Clayton

FOR MY MOM AND DAD
THANK YOU!

AN AWESOME BOOK OF THANKS!

BY DALLAS CLAYTON

two lions

THERE DIDN'T USE TO BE BOATS

THERE DIDN'T USE TO BE CARS

THERE DIDN'T USE TO BE PEOPLE

THERE DIDN'T USE TO BE STARS

THERE DIDN'T USE TO BE ANYTHING

THANK YOU TO THE SUN ABOVE

THANK YOU
FOR MY FRIENDS
I LOVE

THANK YOU FOR THE EARTH AND AIR
THANK YOU FOR THE FOOD TO SHARE

AND FOR THE BREEZE AND FOR THE RAIN

AND DESERT DRY

AND MOUNTAIN STEEP

AND FOXES
DACHSHUNDS
OXEN
SNAKES

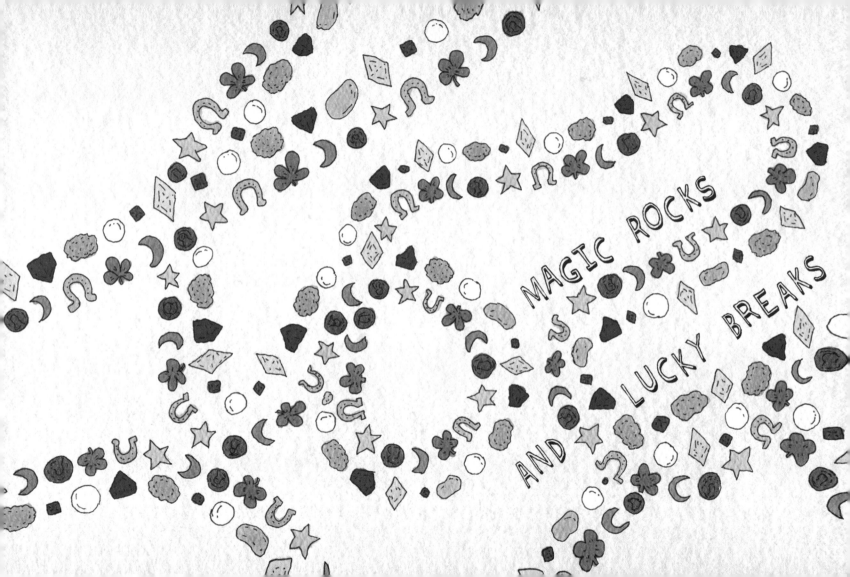

MAGIC ROCKS AND LUCKY BREAKS

HAVING ALL THE TIME IT TAKES
AND BOXES FOR PRETEND

AND BALLS TO KICK
AND KITES TO FLY

AND PLACES TO GO
WHEN YOU WANT TO CRY

SKIPPING ROPE WITH JUNGLE CATS

AND ALLIGATOR ACROBATS

THANKS TO THEM
THEY'RE ALL
SO GREAT

AND THANKS
TO CITIES
AND COUNTRIES TOO

LIKE AUSTRALIA

AND SWEDEN

AND FRANCE

AND PERU

MN

MO

MT

SE

FR

NV

AU

PE

AND TO PLANETS
LIKE SATURN
AND VENUS AND MARS

I'VE NEVER BEEN THERE

BUT THEY DON'T SEEM SO FAR

TO MOMS AND DADS AND SISTERS AND BROTHERS

TEACHERS AND DOCTORS AND ARTISTS AND OTHERS

WHO MAKE ALL OUR LIVES SO MUCH BETTER FOR LIVING

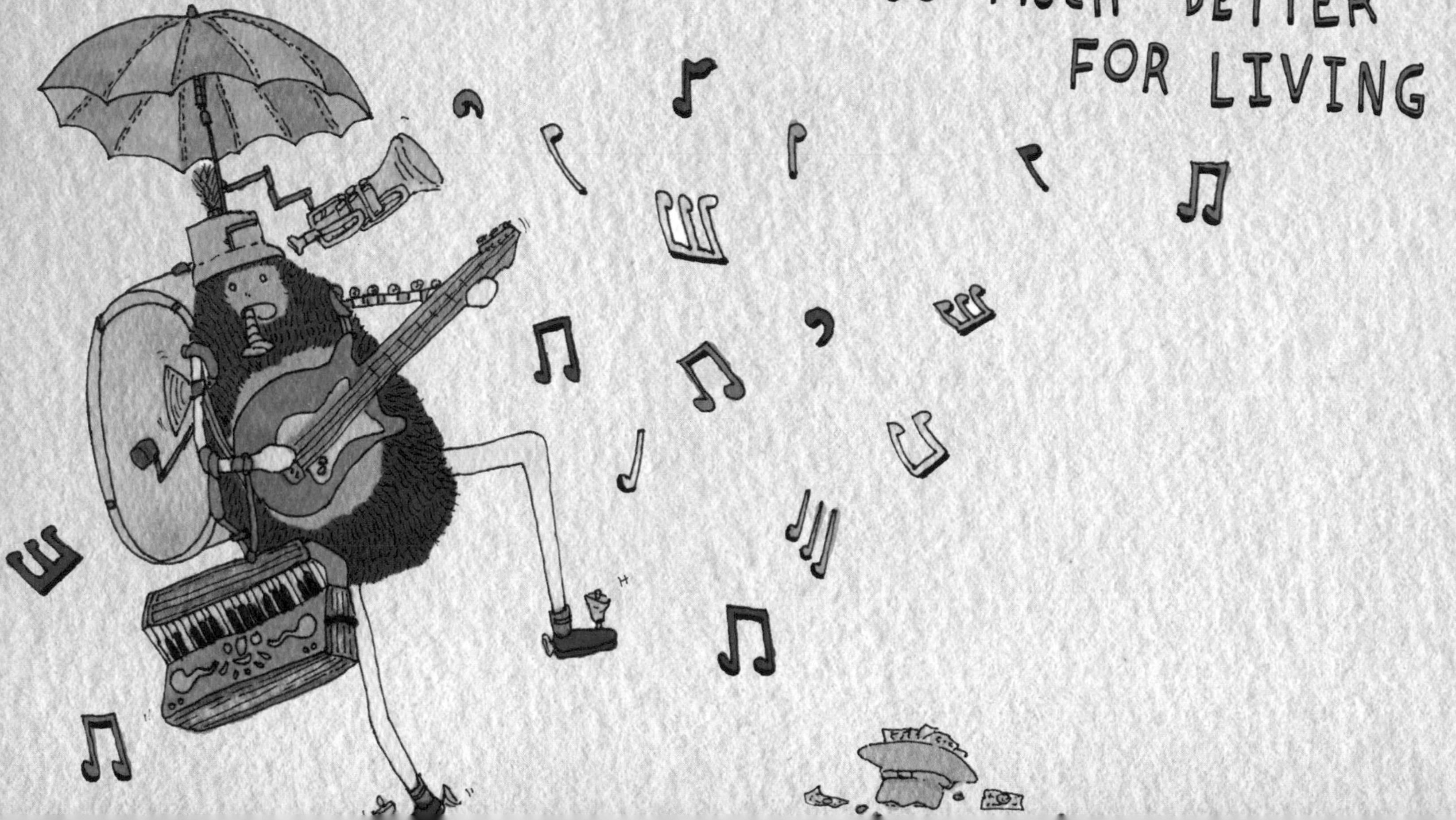

THANKS TO MUSIC

AND DANCING

AND SINGING

AND GIVING

IT'S SO EASY
WE SEE THESE THINGS
EVERY DAY

TO FORGET
TO SAY THANK YOU
IN EVERY WAY

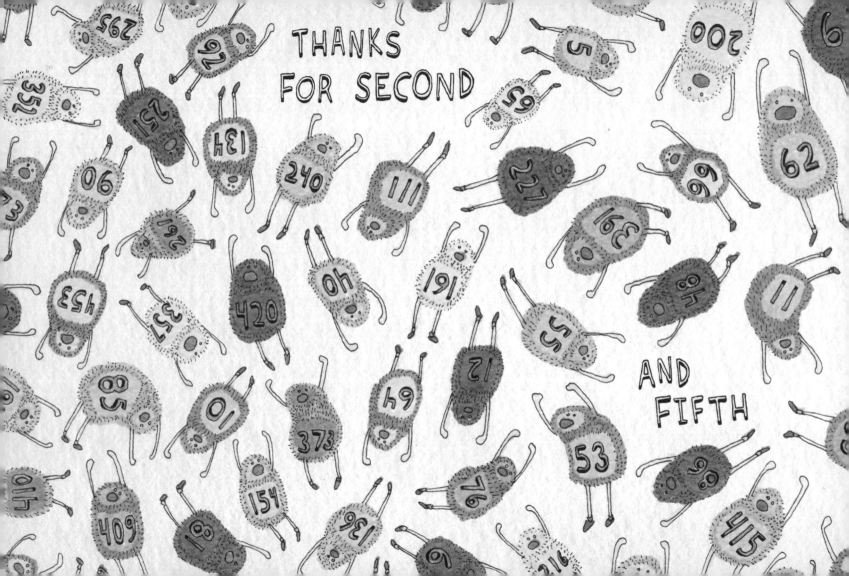

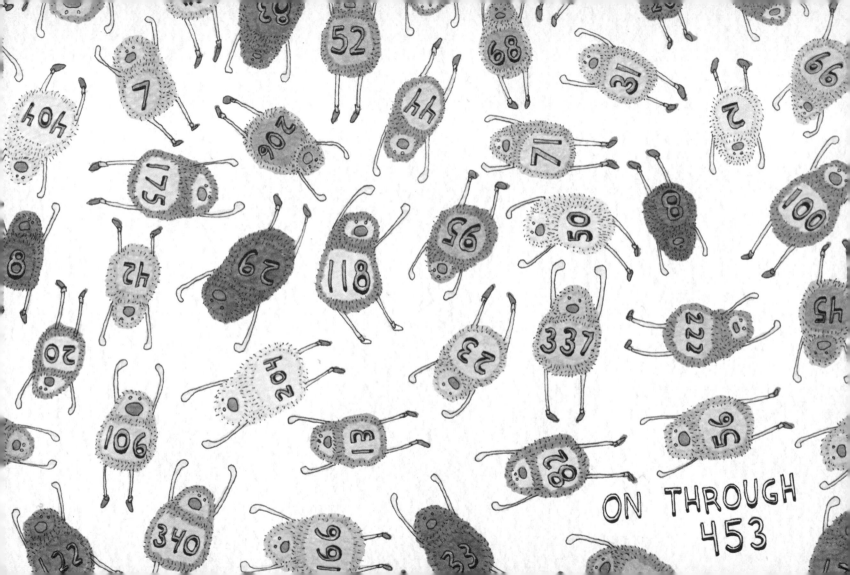

ON THROUGH 453

LIKE GIGANTIC
DINO
MACHINES

AND TO
SMALL THINGS

AND ALL THINGS

THAT FALL
IN BETWEEN

EVEN BAD THINGS

THAT TURN
"COULDN'TS"
TO "COULDS"

THANK YOU TO THOSE
FOR THEY MAKE US ALL STRONGER

THEY MAKE US
ALL SMARTER

THEY MAKE US
LAST LONGER

NEW THINGS
THAT CAN CLIMB UP
SO HIGH IN THE RANKS
THAT WE THANK THEM
WITHOUT EVEN TELLING THEM "THANKS"

THANK YOU TO ALL
THAT HAS EVER EXISTED
AND EVERYTHING ELSE
I COULD NEVER HAVE LISTED

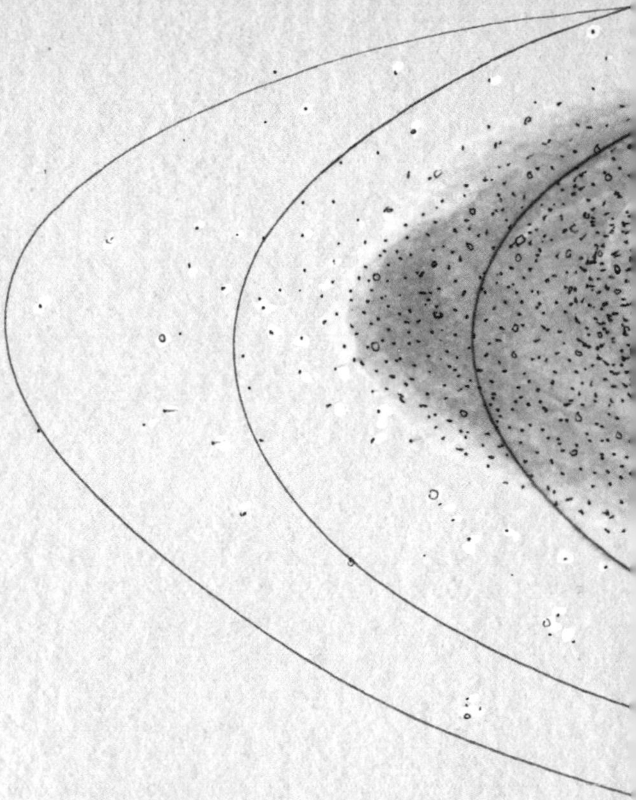

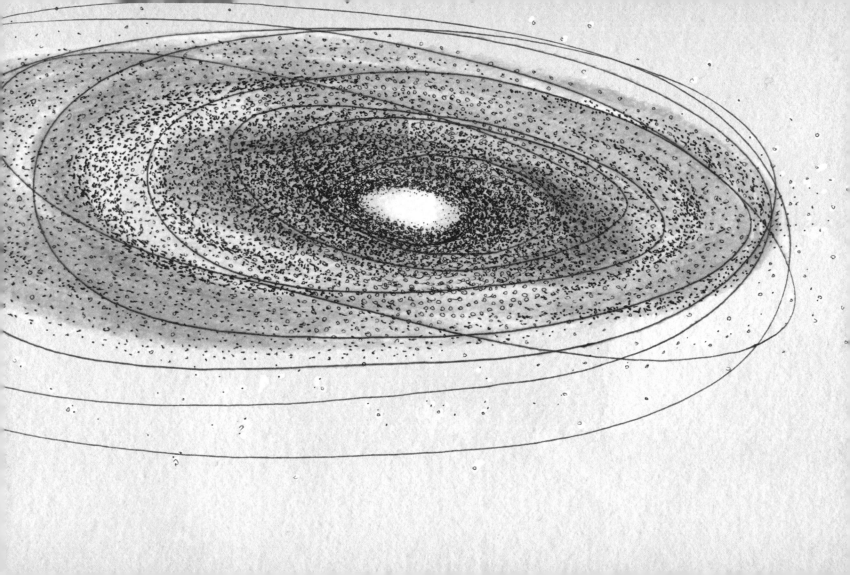

THERE DIDN'T USE TO BE THANK YOUS
SO THANK YOU FOR THOSE
THANK YOU IN LANGUAGES I DON'T EVEN KNOW
MERCI
GRAZIE
DIOLCH
DANKE

THANK YOU WITH KISSES
AND THANK YOU WITH HUGS
FROM A PART OF MY HEART
THAT IS SO FULL OF LOVE

I SAY "THANK YOU" TO YOU
JUST FOR BEING YOURSELF

YOURSELF'S AS IMPORTANT
AS ANYTHING ELSE

SO THANK YOU MY CHILD
AS YOU READ THESE LAST LINES

REMEMBER TO "THANK YOU"
WHEN SOMEONE IS KIND

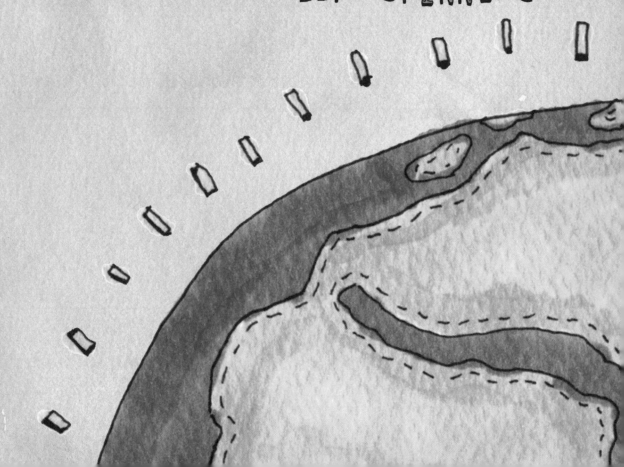

BECAUSE THANK YOUS ARE WHAT MAKE
THIS WHOLE WORLD KEEP SPINNING

AND THANKS NEW BEGINNING

DALLAS CLAYTON IS THE AUTHOR AND ILLUSTRATOR OF AN AWESOME BOOK. HE IS ALSO THE CREATOR OF THE AWESOME WORLD FOUNDATION WHICH DONATES BOOKS TO CHILDREN IN NEED. DALLAS HAS TOURED THE PLANET READING TO THOUSANDS OF KIDS, GIVING AWAY BOOKS AND ENCOURAGING THEM TO DREAM BIG.

HE LIVES WITH HIS FAMILY ON A UNICORN RANCH IN SOUTHERN CALIFORNIA AND SPENDS HIS DAYS WORKING ON HIS TIME MACHINE.